BRING
BACK
THE
DEER

BRING
BACK
THE
DEER

Written by JEFFREY PRUSSKI
Illustrated by NEIL WALDMAN

GULLIVER BOOKS
HARCOURT BRACE JOVANOVICH
San Diego   Austin   Orlando

HBJ

Requests for permission to make copies of
any part of the work should be mailed to:
Permissions, Harcourt Brace Jovanovich, Publishers,
Orlando, Florida 32887.

Library of Congress Cataloging-in-Publication Data

Prusski, Jeffrey John.
Bring back the deer.

"Gulliver books."
Summary: A young brave's hunting ritual, in which
he pursues a deer through the winter forest, brings him
to an understanding of his identity and inner strength.
1. Indians of North America—Juvenile fiction.
[1. Identity—Fiction. 2. Indians of North America—Fiction]
I. Waldman, Neil, ill. II. Title.
PZ7.P94963Br   1988   [E]   86-33605
ISBN 0-15-200418-1
First edition
A B C D E

The illustrations in this book were done in Prang watercolors
on 140 lb. d'Arches cold pressed paper.

The display type was set in ITC Goudy Sans Book

The text type was set in ITC Berkeley Oldstyle Book

Composition by Thompson Type, San Diego, California

Color separations were made by Bright Arts, Ltd., Hong Kong.

Printed and bound by Tien Wah Press, Singapore

Production supervision by Warren Wallerstein and Rebecca Miller

Designed by Michael Farmer

To Angalicon, Selentir, Salix, Therin,
and as we loved him best,
Allen Atkinson

—J.P.

To Erin Gathrid,
who gave me the wonderful opportunity
to illustrate my first picture book

—N.W.

WINTER WAS NOT AN EASY TIME. The great summer camps were broken. People scattered into clans and even into single family bands. When food is hunted and gathered only the bounty of summer can support large numbers in a small area.

And so it was that winter found the boy's family inside their skin lodge, camped alone in a clearing deep in the forest. With Grandmother's help, the boy's sister had been brought into the world early that morning. The boy's mother rested, not yet ready to travel, and his father had gone hunting. It was up to the boy and his grandfather to look after the family.

The boy's grandfather did not hunt now. He was old, and white hair fell to his shoulders. Many winters had carved his face. Their people sought him out for his counsel. Waiting by the fire, Grandfather took no notice of their approach. Then he would turn and beckon to them, his eyes reflecting the light of the fire.

It was said that in dreams he walked many lands. And many things were made clear to him. "Heed your dreams," he would say. "Welcome them. For they are the greatest teachers."

Within the lodge, Grandfather sat before the fire and spoke to the boy. The labor of imparting wisdom to the young fell upon the old, then as now. It was not an easy task.

"The fire is important to our people and to the telling of tales," said the old man. "The light, the heat, and the sounds of burning wood speak to our spirits more deeply than any words."

The old man paused. "Winter is a time for stories, and one should call upon the fire to join in the telling of the tale."

"Shouldn't my father have returned by now?" the boy interrupted.

"Shouldn't you be listening to your grandfather?" scolded the old man.

"I, too, am worried," said the boy's mother. "He has been gone two nights, and there is very little food."

"We have need of the deer," Grandmother spoke. The eyes of his elders met, but no one looked to the boy.

"I will hunt," said the boy, trying to sound brave. "I will bring back the deer."

And the distant howl of a wolf was carried to their ears by a brittle wind.

"So, you will seek the deer." The old man faced his grandson. "This gladdens my heart." He opened the leather pouch that was always at his side and spread its contents before him.

Beginning the ancient ritual, the old man spoke, "To hunt the deer, you must know him. To know the deer, you must be one with him. You must see what he sees, hear what he hears. You must walk as the deer walks. You must become him."

He painted the boy's face, a single white line on each cheek.

"To hunt the deer you must rid yourself of all that is from man: the smell of man, the food that man eats, the thoughts a man thinks. When you become the deer, you will know the deer, and the deer will know you. He will give himself to you. It is a sacred thing."

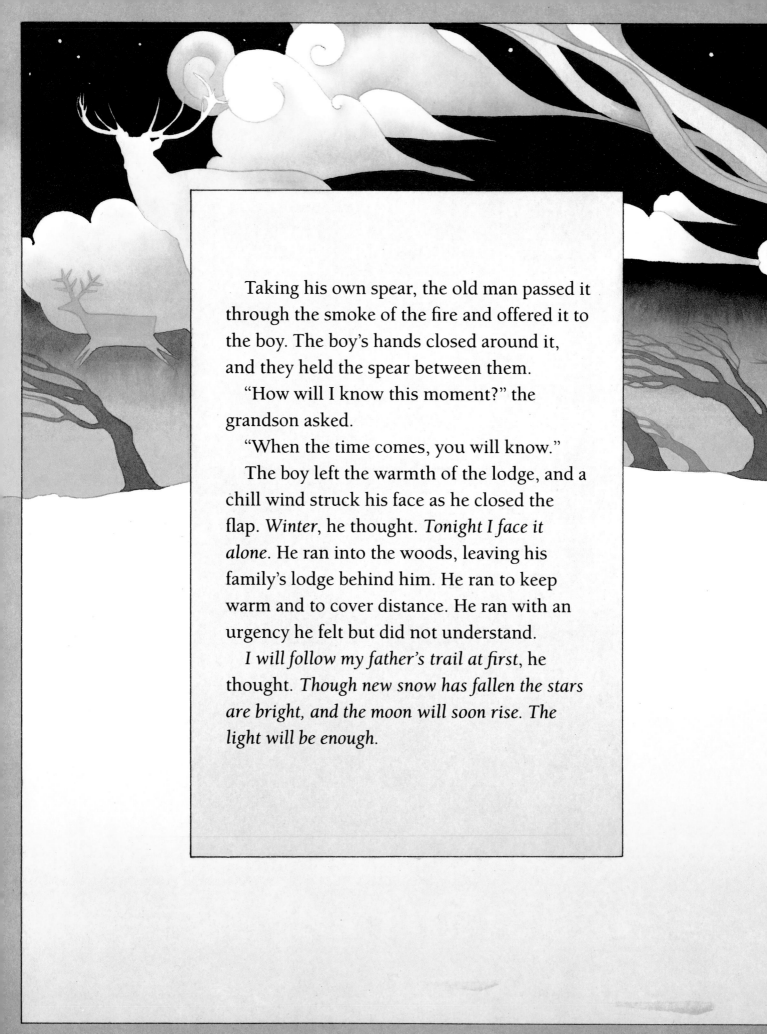

Taking his own spear, the old man passed it through the smoke of the fire and offered it to the boy. The boy's hands closed around it, and they held the spear between them.

"How will I know this moment?" the grandson asked.

"When the time comes, you will know."

The boy left the warmth of the lodge, and a chill wind struck his face as he closed the flap. *Winter*, he thought. *Tonight I face it alone*. He ran into the woods, leaving his family's lodge behind him. He ran to keep warm and to cover distance. He ran with an urgency he felt but did not understand.

I will follow my father's trail at first, he thought. *Though new snow has fallen the stars are bright, and the moon will soon rise. The light will be enough.*

For some distance his father's trail was clear. It moved deeper into the forest where the deer would be less wary. After a time the trail became confused.

I have lost my father's footprints, he thought. *Should I go on seeking the deer? Or should I retrace my steps and try to recover my father's trail? But here—tracks of a wolf! I am not the only one seeking the deer this night.*

He read the tracks. The wolf was large and his gait the measured pace of a hunter, the hind foot placed exactly in the print of the front foot. The boy circled the area but could find no other signs.

A lone wolf it seems, cast out from the pack. Or perhaps he chooses exile.

The boy recalled his grandfather's words. "The customs of the wolf are as complex as those of our own people," he had said. "Wolves speak their own language, though some men are said to understand it. They choose leaders and plan their hunts. They mark their territory and respect the boundaries of other packs. They do not make war on their own kind, nor on man. They take only what they need to live. They mate for life and pass their knowledge on to their young. Learn well the lesson of the wolf."

To survive alone in winter this wolf must be wise, the boy mused. *I will follow him. I will learn the ways of the wolf as my father and grandfather have done.*

And he trotted on, following the new trail.

The boy came to a frozen stream. The wolf's tracks were lost on the windblown ice. He crossed to the other side, steadying himself with his spear, and walked down the bank, following the current that flowed under the river's solid surface.

The water moves more quickly here, and the ice is thinner. Perhaps a deer would come to drink? What is that? Hey-ya! The wolf!

Startled, he fell backward and broke through the ice. The water was not deep, but it was cold and swift.

I've lost the spear! Carried away under the ice. Gone.

The wolf looked on.

I've never been this close to a wolf, thought the boy. *That look in his eyes—he studies me!*

The animal drew back, and the boy crawled onto the bank. He stood up slowly, never taking his eyes off the wolf. He was wet and cold. Suddenly there was a noise—a cracking of branches—and something bounded away through the nearby forest.

It could only be the deer, he thought. Remembering the wolf, he turned. But the wolf had heard the sound as well and was already gone—a flash of shadow in the night, of silver between the trees.

I should go, thought the boy, *but I've lost my spear. How am I to hunt? Must I return? Where is my father?*

The boy stood shivering. The only sound in the forest was that of the water as it dripped from his shirt onto the ground.

"Bring back the deer," Grandmother had said. "This is something you must do."

The boy thought about his grandmother. The way she sat, never wasting a movement, never wasting a word. Watching everything. Like an owl, her head would turn, and her eyes would see. Even in darkness.

She seemed never to sleep, only to sit quietly in the night. Whenever he awoke, she was there in the red light of the fire. She would look at him, a smile spreading across her ancient face, and he would go back to his rest.

If I went back now, without my spear, without the deer, she would not speak, he thought. *But how she would look at me! I will go on. I must not go home without the deer.*

His mind raced ahead, and he began to move in the direction the wolf had run. He passed among the frozen trees, and the light of the moon rose behind him, casting his shadow on the snow.

There! A buck! He is big and by those antlers, an old man of the forest. The boy's excitement grew.

I still have my knife. Perhaps if I can get closer. . . . Quietly now. Move when the wind will cover my sound. Be patient. Move when he moves. Wait when he waits. Closer.

He reviewed all he was taught as he stalked his prey. The moon rose higher. As he waited, the boy became aware that he was not alone. The wolf was also approaching the deer.

Begone, he cursed silently. *This buck is mine.*

At that moment, the deer saw the wolf and bolted toward the hidden boy—toward him and then right past him. The boy spun about and frantically gave chase. He knew this was his only chance.

He is so fast, so fast. How can I hope to catch him? I must run. Run! The deer holds his way before me. And I must run.

Tree branches whipped his face.

Faster, he panted. *I must run faster.*

Heading back through the frozen trees, the deer ran. The boy followed, his heart pounding with the effort.

I have my knife . . . . Running . . . . The moon is rising. I see his antlers cradling the moon. Cradling the moon as he runs. As I run . . . . I run.

The boy's knife fell from his hand.

My knife! I don't need it. I can run faster . . . . Faster . . . . We are heading toward the stream.

In one great leap he is across.

In one great leap . . . I, I am across. Running . . . . Running on four legs! My antlers cradling the moon. Cradling the moon as I run.

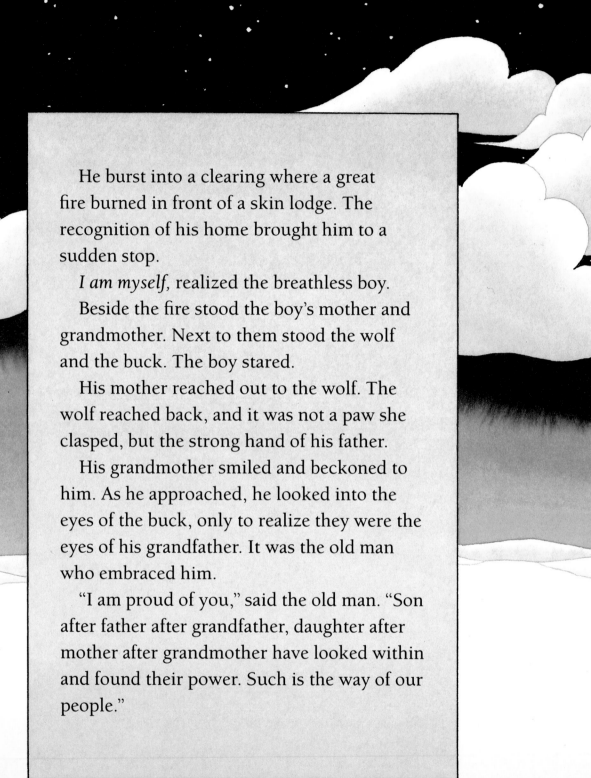

He burst into a clearing where a great fire burned in front of a skin lodge. The recognition of his home brought him to a sudden stop.

I am myself, realized the breathless boy.

Beside the fire stood the boy's mother and grandmother. Next to them stood the wolf and the buck. The boy stared.

His mother reached out to the wolf. The wolf reached back, and it was not a paw she clasped, but the strong hand of his father.

His grandmother smiled and beckoned to him. As he approached, he looked into the eyes of the buck, only to realize they were the eyes of his grandfather. It was the old man who embraced him.

"I am proud of you," said the old man. "Son after father after grandfather, daughter after mother after grandmother have looked within and found their power. Such is the way of our people."

They stood in silence, watching the fire burn. From inside came a baby's soft cry.

I wonder what my sister will bring back to us when it is her time, thought the boy.

The family entered the lodge, taking shelter from the winter night. Soon they must be on their way.